Hansel and Gretel

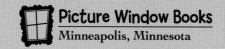

Picture Window Books
Minneapolis, Minnesota

First published in the United States in 2010
by Picture Window Books
151 Good Counsel Drive
P.O. Box 669
Mankato, Minnesota 56002
www.picturewindowbooks.com

©2005, Edizioni El S.r.l., Treiste Italy in HANSEL E GRETEL

Printed in the United States of America.

All books published by Picture Window Books
are manufactured with paper containing
at least 10 percent post-consumer waste.

Library of Congress Cataloging-in-Publication Data
Piumini, Roberto.
[Hansel e Gretel. English] Hansel and Gretel / by Roberto Piumini; illustrated by Anna Laura
Cantone.
p. cm. — (Storybook classics)
ISBN 978-1-4048-5500-7 (library binding)
[1. Fairy tales. 2. Folklore—Germany.] I. Cantone, Anna Laura, ill. II. Hansel and Gretel. English.
III. Title.
PZ8.P717Han 2010
398.2—dc22
[E]
2009010422

Hansel and Gretel

Retold by Roberto Piumini
Illustrated by Anna Laura Cantone

Once upon a time, a boy named Hansel and a girl named Gretel lived near a large forest with their father and stepmother. The father was a woodcutter, and they were very poor. The four of them had nothing to eat.

One night, the stepmother whispered to the woodcutter, "Husband, you must take the children into the woods and leave them there! They can live on the blueberries that grow there. Then we will have enough bread for ourselves!"

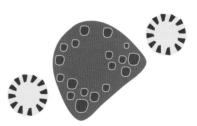

The father did not want to abandon his children, but the stepmother insisted. So one morning he took his children into the woods.

Hansel, who had overheard his stepmother talking the night before, had filled his pockets with white pebbles. Every five steps he dropped one on the path.

When they were in the middle of the woods, their father said, "Wait here, I'll be back in a moment."

But, of course, he didn't come back.

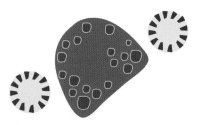

The children found their way home, pebble by pebble. When their stepmother saw them, she scowled, but their father was overjoyed that they had returned.

Later that night, the stepmother whispered to her husband, "We will all surely starve! It's best for everyone if you leave them behind in the forest."

Again, Hansel heard his stepmother's plan. He tried to leave his room to look for more pebbles, but the door was locked. The next morning, the father took his children into the woods again. This time, Hansel dropped bread crumbs along the way to mark the way home.

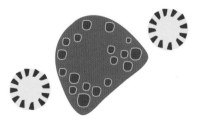

Once they were deep within the woods, the father said, "Wait here, I'll be back in a moment."

But, of course, he didn't come back.

"We'll just follow the bread crumbs to find our way back home!" said Hansel.

But the crumbs had disappeared. They had been carried away by the ants and eaten up by birds.

The children were completely lost, and night was coming.

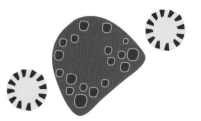

Hansel and Gretel walked and walked all night and into the next day. On the evening of the second day, they saw a little house. When they walked up to it, they realized that it was made of candy!

Hungry and tired, they started nibbling on the sugar windows.

Suddenly, the door opened and out came a friendly old woman — or so they thought.

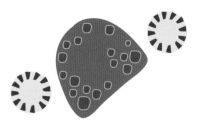

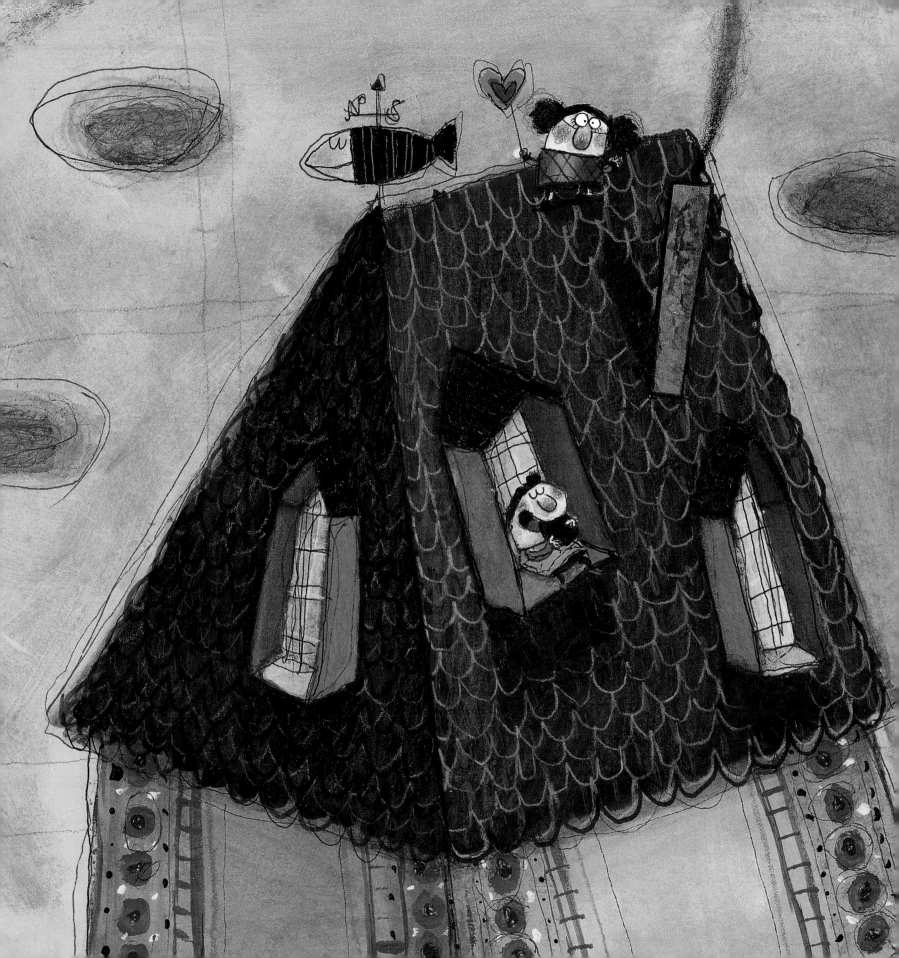

The woman was pleased to see two children at her home. "What lovely children!" she cried. "Please come in, the food is even better inside!"

So Hansel and Gretel went inside. The old woman made a delicious supper for them. Then she gave them a bed to sleep in.

But as soon as they were asleep, she grabbed Hansel and locked him in a cage. The old woman was, in fact, an evil witch in disguise. She had lured the two children inside with her candy house and her sugar windows.

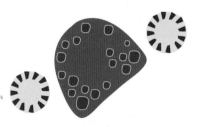

In the morning, the witch said to Gretel, "Go and make a meal for your brother to fatten him up. When he's nice and plump, I'll eat him!"

Gretel cried and pleaded, but there was nothing she could do. So she made a meal for her brother.

As the days went on, Gretel made Hansel meal after meal. Hansel became fatter and fatter while Gretel had only bread and water to eat.

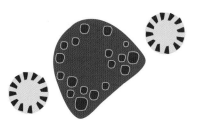

The witch's eyesight was not very good, and she could never tell if Hansel was fat enough to eat. So every day she ordered Hansel, "Stick your finger out so I can feel how plump you've become!"

Instead, Hansel stuck out a twig.

When the witch felt it, she grumbled, "You eat all the time, yet you don't get any fatter!"

Desperate to plump him up, she had Gretel feed him more and more food.

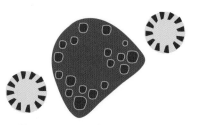

few weeks later, the witch felt the twig again and became impatient. "That's it!" she said. "Whether you are fat or thin, I'm going to eat you right now. Light the fire, Gretel!"

The little girl cried and cried as she lit the fire. "Have you lit the fire yet, Gretel?" screeched the witch.

"No," cried Gretel. "The old, rusty door won't open!"

"Then get out of the way. I'll open it myself!" yelled the angry witch.

But as soon as she opened the door, Gretel shoved the witch into the oven and trapped her inside forever.

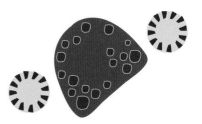

Gretel opened the cage and let Hansel out. The boy had become as plump as a piglet.

Hansel and Gretel hugged each other, and then they gathered up all of the witch's treasures and went back to the forest. They walked and walked until they found a path they recognized, and soon they had found their way home.

The two children hid outside the house, worried that their stepmother would see them. But their father had felt so guilty for listening to her and abandoning his children that he had sent her away. When Hansel and Gretel realized that their stepmother was gone forever, they ran to meet their father.

The woodcutter hugged and kissed his children over and over again.

And the three of them went on to live rich and happy lives.

1. Why do you think the father agreed to leave Hansel and Gretel in the forest?

2. Hansel and Gretel dropped first pebbles, then bread crumbs to find their way back home. What other small things could they have dropped?

3. The witch's house was made of candy, and the windows were made of sugar. What do you think the roof was made out of? What about the door and other parts of the house?

4. Hansel and Gretel were happy to see their father. Were you surprised that they forgave him?

Glossary

abandon (uh-BAN-duhn)—to leave forever

desperate (DESS-pur-it)—willing to do anything to change a situation

disguise (diss-GIZE)—dressed in a way that hides who someone really is

guilty (GIL-tee)—if you feel guilty, you feel bad because you have done something wrong

impatient (im-PAY-shuhnt)—in a hurry and unable to wait

insisted (in–SIST-id)—demanded something very strongly

lured (LOORD)—tricked someone into a trap

scowled (SKOULD)—made an angry frown

starve (STARV)—to be hurt or die from going without food

Write Your Own Fairy Tale

Fairy tales have been told for hundreds of years. Most fairy tales share certain elements, or pieces. Once you learn about these elements, you can try writing your own fairy tales.

Element 1: The Characters

Characters are the people, animals, or other creatures in the story. They can be good or evil, silly or serious. Can you name the characters in *Hansel and Gretel*? There are Hansel, Gretel, their father, their stepmother, and the witch.

Element 2: The Setting

The setting tells us *when* and *where* a story takes place. The *when* of the story could be a hundred years ago or a hundred years in the future. There may be more than one *where* in a story. You could go from a house to a school to a park. In *Hansel and Gretel*, the story says it happened "once upon a time." Usually this means that it takes place many years ago. And *where* does it take place? Their home, the forest, and the witch's house.

Element 3: The Plot

Think about what happens in the story. You are thinking about the plot, or the action of the story. In fairy tales, the action begins nearly right away. In *Hansel and Gretel*, the plot begins on the first page. The stepmother whispers, "Husband, you must take the children into the woods and leave them there." And the story takes off from there!

Element 4: Magic

Did you know that all fairy tales have an element of magic? The magic is what makes a fairy tale different from other stories. Often, the magic comes in the form of a character that doesn't exist in real life, such as a giant, a talking animal, or in the case of *Hansel and Gretel*, a scary witch.

Element 5: A Happy Ending

Years ago, fairy tales ended on a sad note, but today, most fairy tales have a happy ending. Readers like knowing that the hero of the story has beaten the villain. Did *Hansel and Gretel* have a happy ending? Of course! Not only did they escape the witch, they also returned to their father, who hugged and kissed them. And as the story says, "the three of them went on to live rich and happy lives."

Now that you know the basic elements of a fairy tale, try writing your own! Create characters, both good and bad. Decide when and where their story will take place to give them a setting. Now put them into action during the plot of the story. Don't forget that you need some magic! And finally, give the hero of your story a happy ending.

Roberto Piumini lives and works in Italy. He has worked with children as both a teacher and a theater actor/entertainer. He credits these experiences for inspiring the youthful language of his many books. With his crisp and imaginative way of dealing with every kind of subject, he keeps charming his young readers. His award-winning books, for both children and adults, have been translated into many languages.

Anna Laura Cantone holds a degree in illustration for children's books from the European Design Institution in Milan, Italy. Many of her works have been translated into other languages. She is the recipient of several awards, including the Andersen Award at the Bologna children's book fair. In addition to books, her work has appeared in specialty magazines. When she's not illustrating, she exhibits her sculptures, paintings, and installations.

More Tales to Treasure

Open a Storybook Classic and experience the world of traditional fairy tales told through simple prose and splendid artwork. These safe and inventive picture books feature beautiful and whimsical illustrations that will charm young and old alike.